Copyright © 2020 Clavis Publishing Inc., New York

Originally published as *Beer wil niet slapen* in Belgium and the Netherlands by Clavis Uitgeverij, 2018
English translation from the Dutch by Clavis Publishing Inc., New York

Visit us on the Web at www.clavis-publishing.com.

Bear Is Not Sleepy written by Jelleke Rijken & Mack van Gageldonk and illustrated by Mack van Gageldonk

ISBN 978-1-60537-566-3

This book was printed in June 2020 at Nikara, M. R. Štefánika 858/25, 963 01 Krupina, Slovakia.

First Edition
10 9 8 7 6 5 4 3 2 1

3 9547 00462 9510

Written by Jelleke Rijken and Mack van Gageldonk

Illustrated by Mack van Gageldonk

Bear Is Not Sleepy

Clavis

NEW YORK

It's almost winter.

Bear is by the tree, eating apples.

"Come play with us, Bear," call Elephant and Chicken.

"I have no time to play," mumbles Bear.

"I have to eat a lot before I go to sleep for the winter."

Elephant and Chicken join Bear.
They see a group of birds in the sky.

"They are flying to a warm place for the winter," Elephant tells Bear.
Bear thinks for a minute.
Why do Bears always have to sleep in the winter?
Maybe he would rather go to a warm place too.

"Where are they going?" Bear wonders.

"Let's follow the birds," Bear tells his friends.
"It's a very long way," Elephant warns Bear.

"Won't you get tired?" asks Chicken.
"I'm not sleepy at all," says Bear. "Let's go!"

So off they go.

They walk until they come to a dark forest.

"Stay close to me," Bear tells Elephant and Chicken.

At the other edge of the forest is a river.

How will they get across?

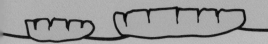

They can use these big leaves as floats!
It's a long way across.
Elephant and Chicken decide to take a nap.
But Bear isn't sleepy . . . yet.

Finally, they reach the other shore.

Which way should they go from here?

Bear and his friends look around.

Then they look up. Hanging from a tree is a sloth.

"Can you tell us which way the birds went?" Bear asks Sloth.

"Oh, I was having such a nice dream," says Sloth.

And before he can answer, Sloth drifts back to sleep.

But Bear isn't sleepy . . . yet.

So, Bear, Elephant, and Chicken walk on.
They cross a great cliff.

They hike through a desert.

They are almost there!
They can see the warm place across the water.
But . . . Bear is finally beginning to feel a little sleepy.

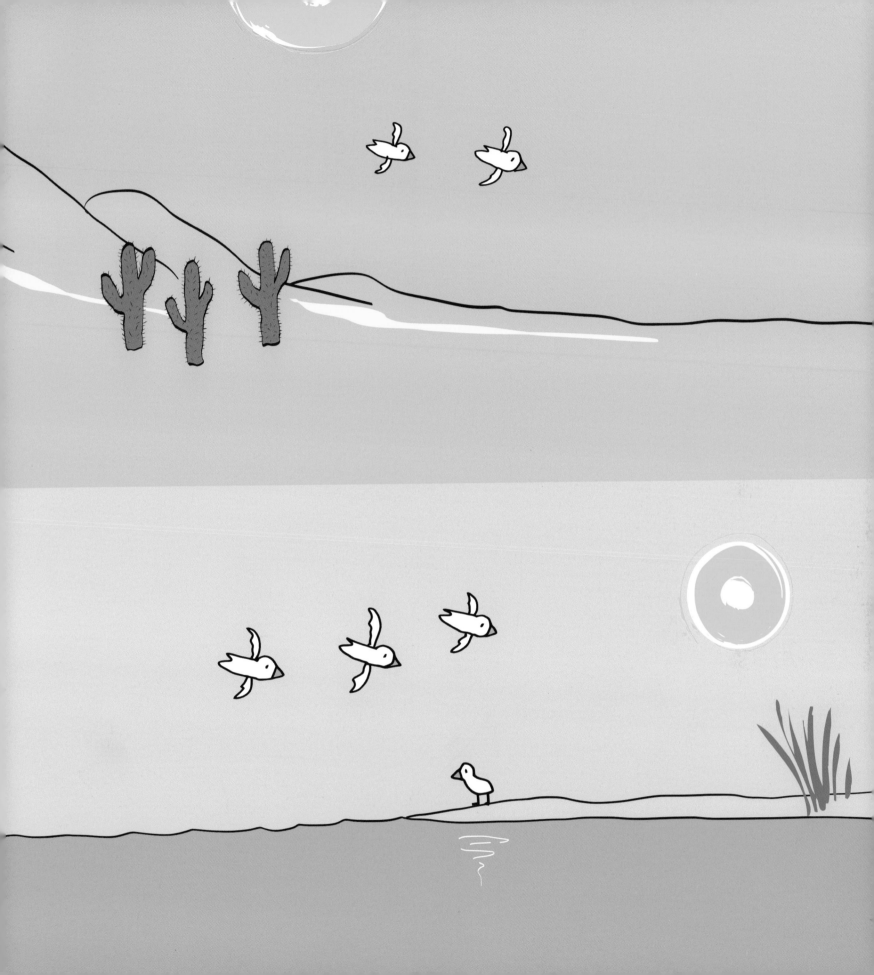

"Come on, Bear," says Elephant.

"Hurry," says Chicken.

Bear doesn't answer. He has fallen asleep.

"Wake up, Bear," his friends say.

"We came all this way."

Bear opens his eyes and starts to cry.

"I just want to go home," cries Bear.

"Bears don't go to warm places in the winter.

Bears sleep in the winter."

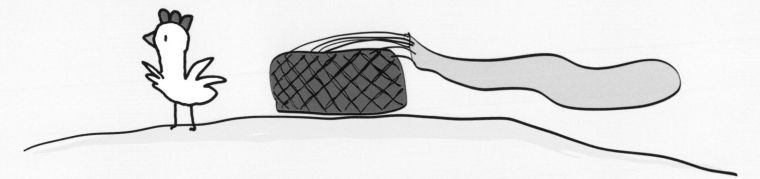

Elephant and Chicken want to help their friend.
"Look. A balloon!" calls Chicken. "We can fly home!"

Elephant blows air into the balloon.

They help each other climb aboard. And off they go!

Bear, Elephant, and Chicken fly over the desert.
They sail over the cliff,
the river, and the dark forest.

They fly home, where Bear finds a nice cozy place to go to sleep for the winter.
Because that's what bears do.